First Flight

First Flight

David McPhail

Blackie

for Brecon
and
for Melanie (After all, it was her idea!)

Copyright © 1987 David McPhail
A *Joy Street Book* first published 1987 by Little, Brown and Company, Inc .,**USA**
This edition published 1988 by Blackie and Son Ltd

British Library Cataloguing in Publication Data
McPhail, David, *1940–*
First flight.
I. Title
813′.54 [J]   PZ7
ISBN 0–216–92337–9

Blackie and Son Ltd
7 Leicester Place
London WC2H 7BP

Filmset by Deltatype, Ellesmere Port
Printed in Great Britain by
Cambus Litho, East Kilbride, Scotland

I'm going to visit my grandmother.
I'm going to fly.
It will be my first flight.

My mother and father drive me to the airport.

I get my ticket . . . find my gate . . .

and go through security.

While I'm waiting,
I watch them get my
plane ready.

When my number is called, I get on the plane.

I find my seat . . .

and put away my suitcase.

I fasten my seat-belt and listen to the safety instructions.

I sit back and relax while the plane takes off.

I look out of the window. The world below is getting smaller.
I think I can see my house.

In a little while lunch is served.

After lunch there's a film.

It's rather sad . . . but it has a happy ending.

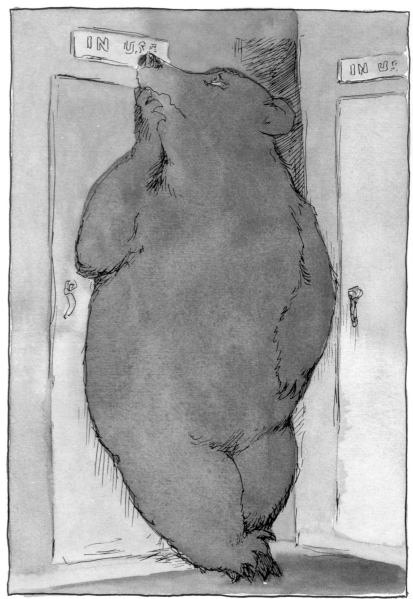

When the film is over, I go to the toilet.

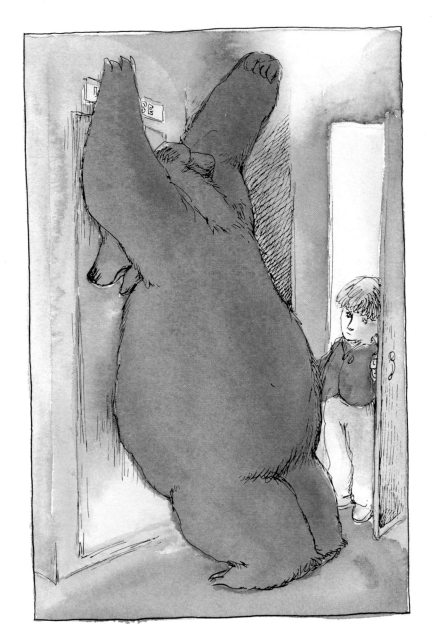

The plane begins to bounce. The captain asks us to return to our seats.

We are flying through a storm. The plane bounces a lot!

The captain calls it 'turbulence'.

When the plane stops bouncing, I read my book.

I'm tired. I go to sleep.

I wake up when I hear something go 'bump'.
It is the landing gear. We are coming in to land.

I check my seat-belt is fastened. Almost before I know it,
we are on the ground.

When we arrive at the gate, I undo my seat-belt and collect my things.

As I'm getting off the plane,
the captain stops me.

He says I have been a good passenger.
He gives me some wings just like his.

My grandmother is waiting for me.

'How was your first flight?' she asks.

'Wonderful!' I say, and I tell her all about it.